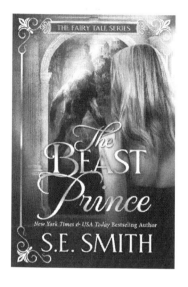

THE FAIRY TALE SERIES

The
BEAST
Prince

New York Times & USA Today Bestselling Author
S.E. SMITH

By S.E. Smith

Acknowledgments

I would like to thank my husband Steve for believing in me and being proud enough of me to give me the courage to follow my dream. I would also like to give a special thank-you to Sally, Debbie, Julie, Jolanda and Narelle, who listen to me, read my stories, and encourage me to be me.

—S. E. Smith

Montana Publishing
Paranormal/Fantasy Romance
THE BEAST PRINCE: THE FAIRY
TALE SERIES

Summary: A cursed prince hopes the
unusual young woman that steps through

an enchanted doorway can break the spell cast upon him before it is too late.

ISBN: 978-1-942562-90-0 (Paperback)
ISBN: 978-1-942562-91-7 (eBook)

Published in the United States by Montana Publishing.
{1. Fantasy Romance. – Fiction. 2. Fairy Tales – Fiction. 3. Paranormal – Fiction. 4. Romance – Fiction.}
www.montanapublishinghouse.com

Synopsis

Lisa Tootles discovers more than she expects when she steps through an enchanted doorway during a game of Manhunt with her cousins. On the other side is a Prince that has been cursed.

Sharden is running out of time. Cursed before he was even born, he waits by the doorway for the one the witch said could break the spell. What he gets is a curvy human woman who doesn't have a clue that his world even existed, much less how to break a curse.

Join Lisa and Sharden as they discovered that it doesn't matter what you look like on the outside; it is who you are on the inside that counts in this delightful fairy tale.

Table of Contents

Chapter 1

Lisa laughed as she ran through the meadow. It was almost midnight, but that didn't stop the fun that had started over an hour before. If anything, it made the game of manhunt even more fun. She and almost a dozen members of her adopted family, ranging in age from four to forty, had decided that sitting around the fire listening to their parents, grandparents, and cousins reminisce about the 'good ole days' was about as exciting as attending a funeral.

Lisa grimaced, that probably wasn't the best analogy to use considering that was the reason everyone was there; for her great grandmother's funeral. Breathless, she slid down behind a large bale of hay and tried to catch her breath. Laying her hand on her stomach, she leaned back against the coarse straw and listened. The funeral today had been drawn out with almost a hundred family and friends attending. What had surprised Lisa was that her grandparents had insisted on having a huge fire that evening at the old cottage that her great-grandmother had owned outside the city of Bath, England.

She stared up at the glittering stars. From the few times that she had been to England, it was a rare occurrence to be able to see them. With a sigh, she grinned and made a wish on a falling star as it flashed across the sky. Closing her eyes, she thought of her wish – to find a place where she felt like she belonged. She opened her eyes and shook her head. At twenty, she knew she still had plenty of time to discover that, but still….

"Oh, crap," she whispered when she heard the sound of footsteps followed by a loud yell and a squeal.

One of her cousins had found another member of her team. Afraid that she would get caught, Lisa held the tiny purse she always carried against her hip and scooted around the side of the haystack before she took off running. She ran down the path, veering to the left when she saw someone with a light up ahead. A short distance later, the path became more overgrown. Slowing to a walk, she glanced back over her shoulder before she shrugged. She was tired and could use the break.

A slight frown creased her brow as she continued down the narrow trail. She didn't remember this path from her explorations over the last week. She was about to fumble for the small flashlight that she had when the path opened up and the full moon overhead shone down on the remains of an old building of some type.

Lisa stopped and stared in curiosity at the crumbling bricks. The only thing left was an arched doorway and the low brick walls. She could see a tree on the other side of it, but what was really strange was that it looked like it was the middle of the day on the other side.

Shaking her head, she briefly looked behind her again and bit her lip before turning to stare at the doorway.

She tilted her head and silently argued with herself for several long minutes before straightening her shoulders in determination. She wasn't a wimp and she didn't need anyone to hold her hand. Clutching the small flashlight in one hand and pulling her cell phone out of the pocket of her jeans, she slowly stepped through the crumbling entrance.

Chapter 2

Sharden stood on the other side of the barren, crumbling doorway – waiting. The witch had told him that the one he sought would come through the entrance. He had his doubts, but he had paid the witch the gold that she demanded for the information she had promised would be his salvation.

His eyes flashed upward to the darkening skies. He could feel the pull of the moon. It wouldn't be full for another two nights, but already the magic of it threatened to engulf him. Two nights to seek the cure that had transformed him nearly a decade ago.

Shaking his head, he muttered a soft curse under his breath. He would have been smarter to have kept the gold for all the good that had come from his meeting with the snarly old woman, he thought as he folded his arms across his chest and stared up at the growing clouds. As it was, he would need to seek shelter at the old inn that he had passed early this morning.

"Come on," he whispered, looking at the doorway of the crumbled remains of the building. "The witch swore that the answer to my quest would be here."

He straightened when he saw the faint movement in the shadows of the doorway. The witch had cautioned him not to go near the building. When he had asked why, the witch just shook her head and mumbled under her breath that the doorway only worked one way.

"Those that come in, may not go out," she whispered in a hoarse voice. "The doorway was closed to the magical world long ago. Only those that belong here may enter, but never exit again. You must accept the one that comes through and the curse will be broken."

"What do you mean 'accept'? Accept what?" Sharden remembered asking in frustration.

The witch grinned and shook her head. "You will see," she had cackled.

Now, Sharden's eyes widened in surprise and disbelief as the curvy figure of a young woman stepped through the opening. Disappointment surged through him. The girl looked… normal. How was she supposed to have the magic to rid him of the curse that had been laid upon him before he was even born? His first change to a werewolf occurred when he was barely fifteen years of age. His parents had locked him away in the dungeon of the palace.

The following morning, he had awoken starving and confused. It was then he learned about the curse placed upon his parents for denying a young, pregnant witch shelter from a terrible storm. His parents had shared their grievous action with him and spent years searching for the witch to beg her forgiveness, but she had disappeared.

Sharden jerked back to the present when the young girl turned back to the doorway. He was about to call out a warning when she hit the invisible wall that sealed the magical world from her own. The force of the shield knocked her backwards. He watched in dismay as she stumbled before falling onto her back in the thick grass. He quickly strode forward when she didn't move.

Kneeling on one knee beside her, he stared down into her face in concern. "Are you hurt, my Lady?" He asked politely.

The girl blinked up at him in surprise… and annoyance. "No," she replied with a grunt. "What the heck just happened?"

"It is the doorway, I fear," Sharden replied. "You came through, but you cannot leave."

The girl stared up at him like he had lost his mind. Sharden shifted uneasily. This was not the way most women looked at him. Realizing that he was still staring at her, he leaned down and slid his arm around her shoulders to help her up. He was surprised once again when she shrugged off his help and climbed to her feet on her own, brushing off the grass that clung to her blue cloth-covered legs.

"Thanks, I got it," she mumbled, pushing a strand of long hair away from her face. "So, how do I get back through?" She asked with a puzzled frown.

"You don't," Sharden replied, handing her the strange cylinder shaped object that she had dropped.

"What do you mean… 'I don't'?" She asked, turning to stare at him through narrowed eyes.

"The witch said that once you enter you cannot leave," he replied in a calm voice.

"Witch?" She asked with a raised eyebrow. "Okay… Someone obviously has lost the few marbles that they had," she muttered before turning away from him.

Chapter 3

Lisa threw another savage look at where 'His royal highness, Prince Sharden' sat watching her. Picking up another rock, she threw it at the door. She barely had time to duck when it bounced back at her. With a snort, she grabbed a branch off the ground.

"You already tried that," he informed her with a sigh. "It knocked you on your lovely rear-end, remember?"

She ignored him. Oh, she remembered alright. In her world, wood didn't conduct electricity. In this world, it did. Her arm still tingled and her butt was sore. Frustrated, she weighed the small limb before throwing it like a javelin at the doorway. This time, she had to dive to the side to keep from getting nailed. She landed on her stomach, knocking the wind out of her. Dropping her head onto her arm, she drew in a deep, gasping breath before losing what precious little oxygen she had pulled into her lungs when she felt the touch of a hand on her shoulder.

"Are you finished now?" Sharden asked in a quiet voice. "The clouds are getting darker and I can smell rain in the air." He paused when he heard Lisa mumble. "What did you say?"

In aggravation, Lisa raised her head and glanced over her shoulder at him. "I said great. Frigging luck!

Let's just add a nice thunderstorm to the misery," she retorted.

"I...," Sharden started to reply when several big, fat raindrops landed on him and Lisa. "It is time to go. We will be lucky to make it to the Inn without getting soaked."

Of course, they didn't make it. Lisa released an exhausted sigh and shivered as the cold rain poured over them. She was riding behind Sharden on a beast that looked like a cross between a horse, an elephant, and a dragon. It had a long trunk like an elephant, the body of a horse, and the feet and tail of a dragon. If Lisa had any doubts that she had fallen down the rabbit's hole, it had disappeared when he led her to the creature.

She buried her face between Sharden's shoulder blades and pressed even closer to his slightly warmer body. She was freezing and she didn't do cold well. It made her crabby, miserable, and did she mention, very, very cranky? She curled her fingers into the front of his soaked shirt, hoping to find some warmth. A relieved sigh escaped her when she felt the heat radiating off of his body.

"Your hands are cold," he commented.

"So's the rest of me," Lisa muttered against his back, before she lifted her head. "How much further?"

"We are almost there," he replied, reining the beast to the right. "I can see the lights from the inn."

"Thank goodness," she retorted through chattering teeth. "I'm about to turn into a popsicle."

Lisa stared over Sharden's shoulder. He was warm and she was so cold that if it had been possible, she would have wrapped him around her without a second thought. Right now, she was too tired, cold, and hungry to care that she was in a strange world and might not have a way home. At the moment, all she cared about was finding a warm, dry place, a nice hot meal, and a soft bed.

"I hope you have money," she said before sneezing. "Sorry. I don't think they'll take mine."

Sharden chuckled. "I have gold," he assured her.

Lisa grimaced. Gold! Shoot! If he was handing out gold, he could spill a little of it her way. She would have rolled her eyes at his statement if they hadn't been frozen.

A mournful groan escaped her when he pulled the beast to a stop and slipped his leg over the neck of the animal so he could slide off. She immediately missed the warmth of his body. The chattering of her teeth could be heard over the sound of the rain. She didn't complain when he reached up and pulled her off the back of the creature.

A young boy appeared out of the shadows of what looked like a barn and ran over to grab the reins of Sharden's horse. Sharden asked the boy a quick question, but Lisa missed it. She was too busy trying to bury her body in the warmth of Sharden's arms.

"They have a single room left," Sharden replied.

"I... don't... car... care," Lisa stuttered. "You... You... can... have... the... floor."

Sharden chuckled. "Thank you," he retorted dryly.

"No... no... no problem," Lisa mumbled.

She gave up trying to talk after that. She felt frozen to the center of her marrow! A soft whimper escaped her when Sharden pushed open the door to the inn and blissful warmth surrounded them.

Thank goodness for indoor heating, she thought as her eyes closed.

Chapter 4

Sharden felt Lisa's sigh of pleasure at the warmth in the room. He swallowed the chuckle that threatened to escape. For the past hour she had practically crawled into his clothes with him. He felt a shaft of regret for her discomfort. In his haste to find the witch, he had left much of his gear back at the palace. He would have missed her entirely if he had not overheard one of the stable boys at the palace speaking of an old witch that his father had run into the day before.

Pushing the memory away, he bent and carefully lowered Lisa to her feet before straightening as a male in his early fifties with dark gray hair and shaggy sideburns stepped up to them. Sharden knew the moment the man recognized him. The touch of fear and the nervous wiping of his hands on the dirty off-white apron he wore was clear that he also knew about the rumors.

"Prince Sharden. Welcome to my humble inn," the man stuttered.

"We need a room for the night," Sharden ordered.

The man cast a curious glance at Lisa before turning back to Sharden. "I've only got one left, my Prince," the man muttered, bowing his head. "It is the largest one, though."

"As long as it is clean, that will be fine," Sharden replied with a wave of his hand. "My lady will need dry clothing."

Sharden turned slightly when he felt Lisa nudge him with her elbow. "And food, preferably something hot," she whispered, looking around at the other occupants in the room.

"And some food," Sharden added.

"Immediately, Prince Sharden," the man said, turning and calling out to a young girl behind the bar. "Food and a clean gown for the lady."

"Why is everyone looking at you so weird?" Lisa whispered, stepping forward when Sharden wrapped his arm around her waist.

Sharden shot a heated glance at a group of men staring at them and shrugged. The look was clear, beware and stay clear. He guided Lisa up the stairs.

"Perhaps because I am their Prince," he murmured.

Lisa shook her head. "You don't look all that scary to me and those guys looked scared," she muttered, turning to stare up at him.

"Then perhaps it is because of the beast I turn into on a full moon," he stated in a calm voice before pulling her through the door as the innkeeper stepped back.

"Say what?!" Lisa exclaimed, turning to stare at him in disbelief as he shut the door.

Chapter 5

Lisa stood staring at the tall man leaning back against the door. He stared back at her with an intense look. She was waiting for him to add… just joking, but it never came.

"Explain your last statement, please," she ordered, shivering again now that she didn't have his body heat to warm her. She glanced around the room. A small fire burned in the fireplace. Walking over to it, she turned her back to the heat and glared at him. "You're joking, right? You don't really turn into one of the horse, dragon, elephant things or anything, do you?"

Sharden snorted and straightened when a soft knock sounded on the door. Lisa watched as he opened the door and took a long white piece of cloth and a tray from the person on the other side. Kicking the door shut with his foot, he walked over to the table set up near where she was standing.

"No, I was not," he replied as he set the tray down before he held out the length of material. "There is a bathroom through that door. I suggest you hurry if you wish for the food to be warm."

Lisa grabbed the material from him and stomped over to the narrow door in the corner of the room. Sure enough, there was a miniature bathroom on the other side when she opened the door. Stepping into it, she glanced at him with a pointed look.

"I'll expect an explanation when I get out," she told him through gritted teeth before shutting the door firmly behind her.

"I expect you will," he muttered just loud enough for her to hear.

Lisa didn't take long in the bathroom. She quickly stripped off all of her damp clothing and arranged them around the small room in the hopes they would dry before morning. She had to admit the bathroom looked like her closet had thrown up.

Turning on the shower, she stood under the spray. Still, as heavenly as it felt, she didn't want to take a chance of missing out on a hot meal.

Stepping out of the shower, she quickly dried off and pulled the billowing white fabric over her head. She looked like a virgin waiting for an offering, she thought with disgust. Picking up her tiny purse, she pulled her comb out of it and pulled it through her hair. She braided it to the side before shoving the comb back into her handbag and opening the door. Sharden was sitting in one of the chairs in front of the fire, staring moodily at it.

"You look like your best friend just told you to take a hike and your dog died at the same time," she commented, walking over to where he had placed their covered dishes. "So, tell me about the beast that you supposedly turn into."

Sharden looked at her before turning his gaze to the fire. "Not supposedly," he said with a slight shrug. "In two days time, you'll discover that."

Lisa sank down into the empty chair and studied his face. "I'm hoping to be home before that happens," she replied in a light tone. "So, do you get all hairy or what?"

Sharden's lips twitched at her curious look. She knew he was expecting her to be all freaked out, but Lisa loved anything supernatural. Halloween was her favorite time of year. She always dressed up in the most creative costumes and the house was decorated to the max. The Haunted House at the theme parks had nothing on her.

"Yes, I get hairy," he said.

Lisa nodded, reaching for the cover of the dish closest to her. "I once saw this guy at the beach that was covered in hair. I swear he had more on him than Bigfoot, who by the way is absolutely scrumptious if you ask me. The guy could totally call me for a date on Friday night and I'd go," she said with a wave of the fork she had picked up. "This doesn't taste half bad."

"I don't believe I know this Bigfoot," Sharden replied, leaning forward to lift the cover over his plate. "He is someone you care about?"

Lisa's fork paused halfway to her mouth before she shook her head and took a bite. "We only went out on one date in seventh grade. His cousin is the Abominable Snowman," she added with a twinkle in her eye.

Sharden looked at her suspiciously. "You are teasing me," he said in a slightly surprised tone.

"Actually, he's a mythical creature that lives in the forest of the northwest," Lisa remarked with a grin. "You looked like you could use it. So, what do you look like when you become this beast? Do you become like this werewolf with big fangs and a bushy tail?"

Sharden paused in disbelief. "You have seen one before?" He asked, leaning toward her. "You know about them? Can you cure me of the curse?"

Lisa's smile died. "No," she murmured with an apologetic look. "I'm still trying to figure out if this is all a dream."

Lisa watched as Sharden set his fork down and sat back in his chair. He stared moodily at the fire, lost in thought. For the first time since this crazy adventure started hours ago, she felt a ping of unease.

"The witch swore that the one that came through the doorway would break the curse," he said in a barely audible voice.

"I don't know if there is anything I can do to help you, but if there is, I'll try," Lisa replied, gently laying her hand on his right arm.

Sharden just nodded. She felt bad there wasn't anything else she could tell him. She didn't know why the witch would have thought she of all people could help someone who turned into a werewolf. Heck, she couldn't even figure out what she wanted to do with her life!

Not as though that was a problem now, she thought as she sat back with an exhausted sigh. *What major I was planning on changing to is nothing compared to figuring out how to get back home or dealing with being in a weird new universe.*

Chapter 6

"Lisa, wake," Sharden whispered.

A reluctant smile curved his lips when she groaned, rolled over, and pulled the pillow over her head. It was obvious their late night before made her loath to wake. Still, he had no choice if they were to return to the palace tonight. He had only one day left before the full moon and wouldn't risk being outside the confines of the walls during his change.

"Go away," she ordered in a muffled voice. "It's still dark out."

This time he didn't bother to hide his chuckle of amusement. Pulling the covers back, he had to step swiftly to the side to miss the foot that kicked out. Unfortunately, he didn't dodge the pillow in time. The moment he let go of the covers to grab it, Lisa pulled them back over her with a muted growl.

"Lisa, we have a long way to travel today, we must leave soon. I thought you might like to have something to eat before we left," Sharden said patiently, trying to pull the covers off her again.

He paused when she pulled the covers off of her head and glared at him. "It isn't that far back to the door," she scowled.

"We are not traveling back to the doorway," Sharden replied in a calm voice. "We are going to the palace."

"Why?" She demanded, sitting up. "Did you sleep the whole night on the floor?" She asked suspiciously when she saw the blanket she had given him hours earlier on the bed next to her.

"Of course not," he retorted in exasperation. "The floor is hard and not very clean. Why would I sleep there when there is a perfectly comfortable bed with a nice warm body in it?" He watched as she pushed her hair out of her eyes and stared at him in silence. He couldn't resist reaching out and touching one rosy cheek. Leaning forward, he hesitated for a brief moment before he bent to press a tender kiss to her slightly parted lips. "You were shivering, if it helps. I could hardly let you freeze or become sick, could I?"

A twinkle of amusement came into his eyes at her dark scowl and the delectable pout to her lower lip. With a snort, she shoved him aside and slipped out of the warm bed. A grumble of displeasure burst from her lips when her feet touched the cold floor.

"I'll be out in a minute," she muttered.

"I will have breakfast delivered," he said.

Lisa just nodded and headed for the bathroom. He rose and walked to the door. Opening it, he saw the girl from last night. He ignored her look of fear and instructed her to have fresh fruit, warm bread, and hard-boiled eggs delivered to their room along with a kettle of hot tea.

Closing the door, he leaned back against it and stared moodily toward the bathroom. Last night had been… nice. Actually, it had been more than nice. He had enjoyed talking with Lisa. She had an unusual sense of humor, was totally unconcerned that he was a prince, and instead of looking at him with fear when she learned of the curse placed upon him, she appeared curious and excited by it. He also liked that she didn't put on airs with him that many of the women who came to the palace seeking his attention did.

He had to admit he had been more than a little surprised when she had tossed the top comforter at him and told him that he could sleep on the floor near the fire before climbing in the bed and pulling the thin sheet over her shoulders. He knew his mouth was hanging open when she turned her back to him and promptly fell asleep. He'd stood gazing down at her for a good ten minutes before muttering a silent curse. Deciding he would deal with the consequences in the morning, he kicked off his boots before lying down beside Lisa and covering them both with thick cover. He was glad when he felt her shivering. Almost immediately, she snuggled back against him. With a sigh, he wrapped his arm around her and fell into a deep sleep.

He jerked away from the door when he heard a soft knock. Opening it, he retrieved the tray from the innkeeper with a short nod and a brief instruction to have his mount readied for his departure. He closed the door just as Lisa came out of the bathroom. She was wearing her outfit from yesterday and was braiding her hair once again.

"The day appears to be clear of rain," he said with a smile. "I hope you are hungry."

He watched as a grimace crossed her face and she ran her hands down over her hips. "Always, if you couldn't tell," she said with a sigh. "I love food and food loves me."

Sharden's eyes ran down over Lisa's curvy figure. A slightly crooked grin curved his lips as his eyes lit with pleasure. Personally, he liked what he was seeing and he definitely liked what he had been holding all night. It was refreshing to find a woman that he could wrap his arms around without fear of breaking.

"I think you look fabulous," he admitted before awkwardly holding up the tray. "Food."

Lisa's eyebrows rose in surprise at his statement before she nodded and walked over to the small table they had used the night before for dinner. He followed her and set it down. They ate in silence, both lost in their own thoughts. Before long, breakfast was finished.

"It is still chilly outside," Sharden said. "The innkeeper's daughter brought a wrap that she made up for you."

"Oh," Lisa whispered, fingering the finely spun wool between her fingers as Sharden wrapped it around her shoulders. "Thank you. I hope you paid her for it. I mean, I would, but I don't have any money that she could use here."

"Of course, I did," Sharden replied. "Come, we have a long journey, but should reach the palace by tonight."

"Okay," Lisa muttered, glancing at Sharden's tight face. "You know, things will work out. My mom always told me that things happen for a reason. Sometimes you don't know why, but they always work out for the best in the end. You just have to be patient."

Sharden paused as he opened the door to their room and looked at her.

"I wish I could believe that," he replied in a quiet tone.

Lisa looked up at him with reassuring eyes. "You can," she whispered.

"How do you know?" He asked in a voice filled with doubt.

"Because my mom told me," she replied in a light voice. "Plus, she's never been wrong. You'll see. If the witch said I could help, some how, some way, I will. After all, a witch should know, shouldn't she?"

Sharden stared at her with a bemused expression before he nodded. "Yes, I guess she would," he said after a short pause.

Chapter 7

They left the inn just as the sun was beginning to rise over the distant hills. This time, Sharden placed Lisa in front of him. He told her it was to help keep her warm, but in truth, he enjoyed holding her.

The innkeeper's wife had packed them a lunch of fruit, bread, and cheeses. They would stop midday to rest his mount and refresh themselves. Setting off at a steady pace, he kept one arm wrapped protectively around Lisa as they rode down the wide lane.

"Your family, tell me about them," he instructed almost a half hour later.

Lisa shrugged. "I have my mom, dad, grandparents on both sides, and a ton of cousins, aunts, uncles, you name it," she said. "My parents adopted me when I was about three. I don't remember much before that. They already had five kids, but took me on as well. My great-grandmother supposedly found me wandering in her garden. My mom and dad were living near here at the time and were given custody of me until one or both of my parents were found. After a two years of searching for my biological parents and no one coming forward to claim me, they were able to adopt me. I was lucky, I had three big brothers and two older sisters who doted on me."

"It sounds like an amazing family," Sharden replied.

Lisa nodded. "Loud, noisy, always something going on," she laughed. "Holidays and get-togethers can be dangerous for the unwary. What about you? Do you have a large family? How did you get cursed?"

"Nay, I am an only child," Sharden said. "My parents were not so welcoming as yours. The kingdom was a dangerous place many years ago and my parents were untrusting of strangers. One stormy night, a young woman came to the palace asking for shelter. The guards took pity on her, but not my father. He ordered her to leave. When she begged my mother to intervene, to at least let her stay the night, she refused. In anger, the woman swore that they would pay for their selfishness. She curse that one day they would know what it was like to want to protect their child and be denied it as she was led outside the gates."

"But, why blame a baby for something the parents did?" Lisa asked, glancing over her shoulder at him. "I mean, I can understand her being pissed at your parents, but you? You didn't have anything to do with their decision."

Sharden shrugged. "A parent wishes to protect their child," he replied. "Perhaps since she felt they were threatening her babe by casting her out into the storm, she thought they should know what it felt like to be powerless. I don't know, and I really don't care. All I know is that for three days each month for the past ten years, I have been cursed to live in dungeons below the palace as a beast."

He could feel Lisa's sympathy. He wasn't looking for pity. He received enough of that each month as his father locked him in the bowels below the castle, a single window and candles his only light for the duration of his change.

"Well, it could be worse," she suddenly said.

Sharden raised an eyebrow in doubt. "How?" He asked.

"You could be sick with a terrible disease that there wasn't a cure for or a million and one other horrible things," she explained, leaning back against him and wrapping her hands over his. "Sure, you change, but only for a few days each month and you still have your parents and a palace and a whole host of other things to be grateful for."

A low chuckle escaped him. He did not know anyone who had ever explained his situation in such a positive way. Bending forward, he pressed his lip against the side of her head.

"Thank you, Lisa," he murmured next to her ear. "It will be interesting to see if you feel the same way tomorrow night."

Chapter 8

It was almost nine that night before they arrived at the palace. Lisa was glad that Sharden had better night vision than her. Then again, she was glad she didn't when she saw the dark shadows of animals cutting through the trees. She had ridden behind Sharden as it grew darker so he could hold onto the sword that was strapped to the saddle. He said that he would need both hands if it came to a fight.

Fortunately, it hadn't. A tired, relieved sigh escaped Lisa as they rode through the entrance to the palace. Her butt was sore and the inside muscles of her thighs were screaming in protest. She was used to going horseback riding. It was one of her favorite pastimes. In fact, she went just about every weekend back home, but she had never spent the entire day on one.

"Thank you," she muttered with a wince as Sharden helped her off the horse-like creature. "Ugh! I'm going to be sore tonight."

"That is a shame," Sharden whispered before straightening as an elegant looking man and woman came down the steps.

"Sharden, your journey was successful?" The man asked, looking at Lisa with a curious gaze.

"Father, mother, I would like to introduce Lisa...," Sharden started to say before turning to look at her with a frown.

"Tootle," Lisa responded to his questioning look. "Lisa Tootle. As you can imagine, I took a lot of ribbing from the kids at school with a last name like that."

"Welcome, Lady Tootle, to Castle Brighten," the king replied.

"It's nice," Lisa responded awkwardly. "It's a pleasure to meet you."

"Lisa is sore and weary after our journey," Sharden said, wrapping his arm around her waist. "We are also hungry."

"I will see her to her room," his mother said, stepping forward. "Go clean up and I'll have a meal prepared for you both."

Sharden paused long enough to brush a kiss along his mother's cheek. "Thank you, mother," he whispered, smiling down when she looked up at him with an anxious expression. "All will be well."

She briefly glanced at Lisa before returning Sharden's smile with a tentative one of her own. "I will see that she is escorted to the family dining room when she has finished freshening up."

Lisa sighed again when Sharden reluctantly released her to walk down a separate corridor from her own. Focusing on where she was walking, she studied the long hallway. Both sides were filled with portraits of men, women, and families. It reminded her of some of the museums back home. She couldn't imagine growing up in a place like this. If her family played manhunt here, they would never find everyone!

"Where are you from, Lisa?" The queen asked in a quiet voice.

"Outside of Bath, England," she said, staring at a display of armor. She jumped when it moved. "My dad is from America, though, the Boston area. Is there really someone in there?"

The queen glanced at the guard. "Yes," she replied.

Lisa turned to look at the guard again. "Must make it a pain if you have to go to the bathroom in a hurry," she mumbled.

The queen looked surprised and glanced over her shoulder at the guard. "Yes, I suppose it would," she remarked with a small, amused smile. "Can you help my son?" She suddenly asked, pausing outside a large set of doors on the left side of the corridor.

Lisa turned to look at her with a serious expression. "I honestly don't know," she admitted. "I'm still trying to figure out if I'm dreaming all of this."

"You're not," the queen replied with a heavy sigh. "I hope that you can help us... him," she added, looking carefully at Lisa. "I fear you are our only hope."

Lisa shook her head. "No, there is always hope," she said. "You just have to believe. That's what my mom always says. She said if you believe hard enough, anything is possible. Of course, she also writes books for kids and works at The

Renaissance Adventures dressed as the Fairy Queen, so who knows if it really works or not."

"She sounds like a wonderful woman," the queen responded.

"Yeah, she is," Lisa replied, stepping into the room after a servant appeared out of the shadows and opened the door.

The room was huge, bigger than most of their house back home. There was a large, four poster bed set against the far wall in a room attached to the one they were standing in. This room held a long, narrow couch, two chairs and several low tables. In front of it was a fireplace large enough for her to stand up in. A row of glass doors lined the far side of the room and led out onto a covered balcony.

"Nice," Lisa said, shifting again.

"I will leave you to freshen up," the queen replied, turning back toward the door before she paused. "I will have someone escort you to the family's private dining room in half an hour."

"Thank you," Lisa whispered, suddenly feeling both exhausted and overwhelmed at the same time.

The queen didn't reply as the door opened again for her and she stepped out. Lisa walked through to the bedroom once she was alone, staring at all the finery. She paused a moment before releasing a tired breath and walked into the bathroom. She was surprised to see a gown that actually looked like it might fit her hanging on a hook just inside the door. Deciding that was a subtle hint to dress in something nicer than jeans and a T-shirt, she quickly shed her clothes and showered. She felt refreshed after the warmth of the water soothed her aching muscles. Drying off, she quickly dressed in the clean clothes that had been laid out for her.

She jumped when she stepped back into the living room area and saw Sharden standing in front of the long row of windows. He was staring out over the gardens that were lit by a series of torches. She couldn't help but admire him. His hair was a dark blonde and cut short. His shoulders were wide and his hips... She swallowed. He had a really cute butt. He stood at least a head taller than her own five feet seven foot frame. She liked that. He had a chiseled jaw, a nose that looked like it might have been broken at least once, and light gray eyes that brimmed with intelligence. She also found him to be reflective, mature, and she really loved his quirky, dry sense of humor.

Deciding she had gawked long enough, she cleared her throat to let him know that she was there. A self-conscious smile curved her lips as she held out the soft blue gown she was wearing. She felt like she was going to the prom all over again. Personally, she thought twice in one lifetime had been enough, though she had to admit the appreciative look that came into his eyes was worth it.

"You look lovely," he said, walking toward her.

Lisa could feel the blush rising in her cheeks and grinned. "I feel like I'm ready for my High School Homecoming dance again," she admitted, fingering the material with her right hand. "I thought she was sending someone to escort me to the dining room."

"I sent them away," he murmured, stepping closer.

Lisa's breath caught in her throat when he reached up and ran his fingers lightly along her cheek. Instinctively, her head turned closer to his touch. She wanted more.

"Lisa," he whispered before his hand slid along her jaw.

Lisa stepped closer at the same time as he did. Their lips connected in a soft kiss that quickly grew heated. She ran her hands up his chest and around his shoulders as his own arms quickly slid down to wrap around her waist. Her lips parted and her fingers threaded through his hair as she responded to his passion.

A soft moan escaped her when he reluctantly pulled back. She hadn't realized that her eyes had closed during their kiss. Her eyelids fluttered for a moment before she stared up at him with a slightly dazed expression.

"I shouldn't have…," he started to say before stopping and releasing a deep breath. "Yes, I should. I want you to know that even though we've just met, you make me feel things that I have never felt before. I want you to know how much it means to me before…"

Lisa lifted her left hand off his shoulder and tenderly brushed his cheek when she saw the sad look that came into his eyes. She stroked the lines at the corner of his mouth with her thumb, a look of concern in her eyes when he closed his eyes. There was something he wasn't telling her; something very important.

"What is wrong?" She asked.

"Tomorrow," he began, opening his eyes to stare down at her again before his voice faded and he shook his head. "Tomorrow, I would like to take you out to see the kingdom."

"I'd love that," she replied. "Sharden, everything will be alright. You'll see. We'll figure out how to break the stupid curse. You have to believe that."

He leaned forward and pressed another hard kiss to her mouth just as a knock sounded at the door. "You make me want to believe," he said in a low voice. "Come, my parents are waiting for us. They are curious about you."

"Great!" Lisa replied with a roll of her eyes. "Only the second day in a strange world and I'm entertaining royalty. Who would've thought?!"

Sharden chuckled. "They will love you as much as I do," he teased, sliding his arm around her when the door opened.

A warm glow swept through Lisa at Sharden's teasing comment. Walking beside him, she felt more like she was floating. Deep in her heart, she knew that things would work out. For the first time in her life, she finally felt like she had found her place in the world.

Chapter 9

Late the following afternoon, Sharden laughed as Lisa discussed the different seasonings the Breadmaker used in his breads. She had fallen in love with the hot, crusty rolls and sweet cream butter combined with a spicy cheese. The smile on his face died as he glanced up at the sky. It would be dark in a couple of hours. Regret poured through him. He only had a few hours left to spend with Lisa. He quickly discovered this morning that the more time he spent with her, the more he wanted.

He knew he should have told her the whole truth, but deep down, he had hoped that she was right, that everything would work out for the best. Suddenly, he wanted to spend the last few hours alone with Lisa. Those precious hours would have to hold him for the rest of his life. Stepping forward, he wrapped a possessive arm around Lisa and gave the Breadmaker a stiff smile.

"I apologize for cutting your conversation short, but we must leave," Sharden interrupted the Breadmaker. "Thank you for your delicious meal."

"My pleasure, Prince Sharden," the Breadmaker said with a pleased smile. "I will send a basket of fresh bread, cream, and cheese to Lady Lisa tomorrow morning."

"Awesome!" Lisa said, pulling away from Sharden long enough to hug the Breadmaker. "Thank you so much!"

Sharden chuckled again at Lisa's enthusiasm and the Breadmaker's suddenly red face. Reaching out again, he wrapped his arm around her waist once more, this time holding on with a firmer grip, and turned them away. They quickly stepped out of the roomy shop and onto the bustling sidewalk outside.

"Where are we going now?" Lisa asked as Sharden helped her onto his mount.

Sharden quickly slid into the saddle behind Lisa. "There is one last place I would like to take you before we return to the palace," he said in a husky voice. "It is the one place I go when I need time alone."

Lisa glanced over her shoulder at him and wrapped her hands over the one he had wound protectively around her waist. He saw the question in her gaze, but he ignored it. He wasn't ready for the magic of the day to end and the nightmare that would be the rest of his life to begin.

Pressing his heels to the side of the beast under him, they quickly traveled out of the village at the base of the hill leading up to the palace and into the countryside. It was a little further than he would have liked to have gone, but he wanted her to see the one place he thought was special before…

"Where are we going?" Lisa asked, bringing him back to the present.

"To the one place I find peace," he murmured, reining the huge animal under them to the left and down a long, tree-covered path. "I found it shortly after my fifteenth year."

The path narrowed and appeared to disappear at the base of a large rock cropping. Sharden dismounted and helped Lisa down. He tightly held her hand and led her to the thick vines covering the front of the rock. Reaching out with his free hand, he pulled the curtain of green vines to the side to reveal a narrow opening. He stepped inside, pulling Lisa through the entrance behind him.

He knew the path by heart as he came here right before and shortly after the 'change'. He stepped lightly through the inky darkness, weaving his way by memory. Soon, the glimmer of light from the other side lit their way.

Stepping out of the cave, he drew Lisa to his side and waited for the magic of this hidden valley to wash over her. It wasn't very large, less than a mile long. In the center was a small hut that he had found and rebuilt. The hut sat near a crystal clear lake that was fed by the waterfall at the other end of the valley. A scattering of trees and tall, golden grass swayed in the light breeze that blew down from the mountain.

"It's so beautiful," Lisa whispered, staring around her with wide eyes. "How did you ever find it?"

"I was scared after the first time I changed," he admitted, turning to look down at her upturned face. "My parents told me about the curse and how they'd hoped it wouldn't come true. I was furious with them. I didn't understand why I should be punished for a deed that was no fault of my own."

"I don't blame you," Lisa whispered, touching his face. "I would have been upset, too."

Sharden turned his face just enough to press a kiss to the palm of her hand. "I ran, thinking if I put enough distance between my parents that it would change things," he continued, turning to stare down at the small hut. "I discovered you cannot run from who you are. I met an old woman along the road. One of the wheels on her cart had broken, spilling the vegetables she was taking to the market to sell. She asked if I would help her. I fixed the wheel and helped her pick up the vegetables, she gave me a few pieces of food and told me to take this path. I did and came to the cliff. I tried to climb it, but the walls were too steep. I finally discovered the entrance hidden behind the vines and it led me here."

"Well, if you think of it," she murmured, gazing down at the valley. "If you hadn't changed, then you wouldn't have run away and you wouldn't have met the woman who told you about the path."

Sharden shook his head. "And if the cliff hadn't been so steep, I would have missed the cave," he added with a chuckle. "You always look at things from a strange perspective, Lisa."

"I know," she replied with a shrug. "Can we go down to the hut?"

"Of course," he replied in a husky voice. "That is why I brought you here."

A light flush rose in her cheeks, but she didn't resist when he began guiding her down the path. The remaining daylight hours were theirs. He planned on making every second they had together, one that neither of them would ever forget.

Chapter 10

The light filtered through the curtains and streamed through the window, waking Lisa several hours later. She blinked sleepily, her hand reaching out to search for Sharden. Her head turned and she frowned when she saw the empty space beside her. Sitting up in the bed, she pulled the sheets up around her and tucked them in as she searched the moonlit room.

Sliding her legs over the side of the bed, she rose, pulling the sheet with her and wrapping it around her toga-style. A frown creased her brow when she saw that the hut was empty. There were only three rooms in it; one bedroom, a small bathroom, and the living/kitchen area. Stepping into the living room, she saw that the fire Sharden had started earlier was now just a pile of embers. Shivering, she walked over to the narrow door and opened it.

The light from the full moon shone down on the lake, making the surface glitter as if a million diamonds had been scattered like bird seed over it. Fireflies danced in the breeze. It was breathtaking except for one thing – Sharden wasn't there. Holding on to the sheet, Lisa stepped outside and looked desperately for Sharden. She could feel a sense of growing panic build inside her when all she heard was the wind in the trees and the distant sound of water from the waterfall.

Turning, she hurried back to the bedroom. Dropping the sheet back on the bed, she quickly dressed. Pulling her dress over her head, she tugged it down over her hips before pulling on her stockings and the low boots. Wiping at the tears running silently down her cheeks, she pushed her hair away from her face.

They had come down to the hut. He had shown her the outside before they stepped inside. By the time they had made it to the bedroom, she had known what would happen next. They had spent the rest of the afternoon exploring more than the house, they had explored each other. The soft caresses turned more desperate, more heated, until they had exploded in a passionate lovemaking that had stunned both of them.

Lisa had stared up at Sharden as he came deep inside her, knowing that they were meant to be together. Locked together, she had held him as he shuddered and collapsed on top of her, mumbling that he would love her forever.

"Remember that," he had urgently told her. "Never forget that you are my heart, my life, my love."

"I love you," she remembered whispering in return. "I love you, Sharden, who you are in here." She slid her hand up between them and pressed it against his heart. "I want you to never forget that."

He had kissed her again as if he would never get enough of her. Over and over again, they had come together as if trying to make the afternoon last for a lifetime. She had eventually fallen into an exhausted sleep in his arms. It was the fear at the thought of never feeling them around her again that drove her forward. She opened the door to the hut, only to fall back with a gasp when she saw a dark figure standing in front of it.

"Oh!" Lisa exclaimed, raising a hand to cover her racing heart. "Who are you? I have to go. Sharden…."

"The young prince has returned to the palace," the old woman said, stepping in when Lisa fell back another step at her words.

"How do you know? Who are you?" Lisa demanded, pushing at

her hair in irritation when it fell forward again.

"Do you love him?" The woman asked, stepping closer.

Lisa scowled at the woman. "What business is that of yours?" She asked suspiciously. "Listen, I don't know who you are, but I really have to go. If you need a place to stay for the night, make yourself at home, but I must go. I have to get to the palace."

"Do you love him, Lisa?" The woman asked again, this time in a softer voice.

Lisa paused, about to tell the woman to just get the heck out of her way, but something held her back. Swallowing, she nodded. Perhaps, Sharden had told the woman something.

"Yes," she replied. "Yes, I love him."

The woman stepped forward again until she was standing eye to eye with Lisa. "Even if he is a beast?" The woman asked in a barely audible voice.

Lisa's eyes softened as she thought of Sharden. "He will never be a beast to me," she whispered. "It doesn't matter what the witch did to him, we'll work it out. It is only for a few nights each month. It isn't like I don't have a few bad days either."

"Did he tell you that on his twenty-fifth year, the curse would become permanent?" The woman asked.

Lisa frowned. "What are you talking about? He said he only

changes during the full moon," she said, confused.

"Until his twenty-fifth year," the woman said. "Then, he would remain a beast."

"But... Why?" Lisa asked, shaking her head in denial.

The woman sighed and started to reach out one gnarled hand before pulling it back, letting it drop to her side. "A curse that is as powerful as the one the witch cast does not come without consequences. The witch realized this after she uttered the spell. She would lose her own child because of her anger. She did not learn her lesson, though. The pain of losing her child was too great a burden and she cast yet another spell, this time sealing the fate of the queen and king's son."

"But… Why?" Lisa asked in frustration. "The Queen and King looked for the young witch to beg her forgiveness."

"Yes, I know," the old woman replied, turning away from Lisa and stepping toward the door. "As I said, all dark spells come with a consequence. Unfortunately, the young witch did not learn her lesson as quickly as the King and Queen."

"Why are you telling me this?" Lisa asked, following the woman as she opened the door. "How can I break the spell?"

The woman glanced over her shoulder at Lisa with a sad smile. "It depends on if the goodness in your heart can overcome the darkness that once filled the young witch's,

Lisa," the woman replied in a quiet voice. "Can you love a beast?"

Lisa watched as the woman stepped outside. Could she love a beast? How could she not if that 'beast' was Sharden? No matter what he became on the outside, he was still the man she loved on the inside. He needed her. That was all that mattered now.

"Yes," she said, stepping through the door. She paused when she realized the old woman was gone. "Yes, I can love him." A smile curved her lips as she felt the power of that love, sweep through her. Her face lit with her determination. Turning, she shut the door behind her. "YES! I CAN LOVE HIM!" She yelled up at the moon. "He's mine! Do you hear me! I LOVE HIM!"

Taking off at a run, she raced to the entrance to the cave. Using her right hand to help guide her, she hurried through the dark tunnel, bursting out through the other side, startling Sharden's mount who was grazing on a patch of grass. Rushing toward the animal, she grabbed the reins and climbed onto the saddle. She turned the mount and kicked her heels, racing down the shadowy path back toward the palace. The wind tugged at her hair and she felt stronger and more confident the closer she got to the palace. She let the animal under her have its head as they traveled down the wide lane through the village. She kept one hand on the reins and the other wrapped in the coarse mane as her knees pressed tightly to keep from falling.

"Go," she breathed. "As fast as you can."

The village flashed by her in a blur as the mount heard her desperate cry. The sounds of its massive feet against the drawbridge and the call of the guard to open the gates were whisked away as she flew by them. Pulling on the reins, she half-jumped, half-fell from the saddle as the heaving animal skidded to a stop at the bottom of the steps leading into the palace. Lifting the hem of her dress, she ran up the steps only slowing when the huge double doors opened and the King and Queen stepped out.

"Sharden?" Lisa whispered in a breathless voice. "Is he…?"

Tears glimmered in both of their eyes. The King nodded his head, wrapping his arm around his wife. Lisa slowed as she stepped up to stand in front of them.

"It is too late," the King replied in a voice laden with sadness.

Lisa shook her head. "It's never too late," she said, pressing her lips tightly together. "Where is he?"

"In the dungeon," the king replied. "Where he will remain for the rest of his life."

"Not if I have anything to do with it," Lisa vowed, stepping past them.

"Lisa, can you…?" The queen asked in a desperate whisper.

Lisa shook her head. "I don't know," she admitted before

straightening her shoulders. "It doesn't matter. I love him. Whatever happens, we'll work it out."

The queen's shoulders drooped and she leaned back against the king. "Be careful," she whispered. "He is hurting."

Lisa nodded. "I won't leave him," she promised, looking at the king. "Can you take me to him, please?"

The king nodded and turned. "Follow me," he instructed.

Lisa swallowed and followed the king as he led her down a series of corridors before pausing at a door that had two guards standing in front of it. Turning, he pulled a set a keys from a loop at his waist. He unlocked the door and stood back. Lisa took a step forward, surprised when he didn't go first, but held out the key ring to her.

"You must go on your own from here," the king advised. "Be careful, if he should attack... There is nothing I can do."

Lisa smiled reassuringly at the king, feeling more confident on the outside than she did on the inside. "He won't," she assured him before turning to look down the long winding staircase.

"The large key will let you into his cell. I hope for my son's sake that this will help him," the king added with a heavy sigh, stepping back from the doorway.

Lisa started down the steps, pausing when she heard the door behind her close and the loud sound of the lock echoed behind her. Straightening her shoulders, she continued down the softly lit spiral staircase. The low moan of an animal in pain echoed softly in the direction she was going, growing louder the lower she went.

"Sharden?" Lisa called out in a gentle voice.

"Lisa! What are you doing here? You must go!" Sharden's anguished-filled voice resonated through the dimly lit area.

"No," she responded, walking slowly to the heavy metal door with two small windows, one near the top and the other at the bottom. "I'm coming in."

"No!" Sharden hissed. "You can't!"

Lisa shook her head. "Yes... I can and I am," she said with determination.

A loud howl filled the air, sending a shiver through her. The goose bumps that formed on her arms were not from fear, but the sound of pain in the mournful tone. She lifted the heavy key and slid it into the skeleton shaped lock and twisted it. The click of the lock disengaging sounded loud in the sudden silence that followed Sharden's outraged cry.

She drew in a deep breath before pulling the door open and stepping inside. She turned just far enough to shut the door behind her. Determined, she dropped the key ring to the floor, wincing when the metal struck the stone. It sounded unusually loud in the large room. She kicked the keys through the narrow flap at the bottom of the door.

Lisa glanced around the area, noting that it had been enlarged to make it into an underground apartment containing several rooms. Her eyes flickered to the metal bars over the row of small windows. Moonlight streamed through them. The light from the moon and a fireplace that was built into the far wall were the only light. A movement in the corner near a bookcase pulled her attention to a small alcove cut into the wall next the fireplace.

"Sharden…," Lisa breathed, taking a step forward before

stopping at the low growl that rumble through the air.

"Stop, Lisa," Sharden ordered in a hoarse voice. "You shouldn't be here."

A tender smile curved Lisa's lips. "Yes, I should be. I belong here, next to you," she whispered. "Especially after this afternoon."

"Don't," Sharden's pain filled voice tore at her. "I... We shouldn't have... I just...."

Lisa took another step closer to the dark alcove, staring into the darkness, willing him to accept that she wasn't going to leave him. Her heart pounded, unsure of what she would see, but also certain that it wouldn't matter. She lifted her hand in a silent plea.

"I love you, Sharden," she insisted. "I love the man inside the covering. Come to me... Please."

A snarl ripped from him when she took another step closer. "NO!" He hissed. "Go! FATHER! Come release her!" He roared.

Lisa stiffened and raised her chin. Her hand dropped to her side and she clenched her fists in defiance. Shaking her head, she stared into the darkness.

"He won't come," she stated with a stubborn tilt to her chin. "He gave me the keys and told me that I was on my own. I'm not leaving, so suck it up and deal with it. I won't leave you. You said that the witch told you that I could help you. Well, I'm here."

Another savage snarl ripped the air before dying away. For several minutes, they stood in silence, neither talking. The only sound was Sharden's heavy breathing before he released a vicious curse. Lisa's eyes widened when first one clawed foot slid out into the faint light of the fire, before the rest of Sharden emerged from the darkness. Light gray eyes stared savagely back at her, daring her to not cringe at the sight of him.

Lisa stared back at the most beautiful creature she had ever seen. Sharden's dark blonde hair had grown long and formed a thick mane. His face had lengthened and his nose was now a series of ridges. His lips were thinner and two long fangs peeked from beneath his upper lip. His face was covered with a light covering of fur that ran down his throat and was visible beneath the opening of the white shirt he wore. He still had the narrow hips, but his thighs looked bigger, more muscular under the thick, dark brown cloth pants he wore. Her eyes rose back to lock with his piercing light gray eyes.

"You are...," she started to say, mesmerized by the beauty of him.

"I'm what? A beast? A monster?" He snarled, turning his face away from her to stare at the fire.

Lisa's heart melted at the tortured grief that was twisted in his words. Walking silently toward him, she lifted her right hand and tenderly touched his jaw. Her fingers feathered along the soft fur, caressing and exploring him as she threaded them into the fur and pulling his face toward her.

"No, the most beautiful man I've ever seen," she breathed, slowly moving closer until she was standing as close as she could without him holding her. Staring up at him, her lips curved into a small smile. "I love you, Sharden. I love you, beast or man. I love all of you," she whispered, refusing to let him look or move away from her.

Chapter 11

Sharden's eyes closed at the sweet feel of Lisa's touch. He knew it was her coming down the steps. A part of him wanted to roar out in triumph even as the other part of him wanted to chase her away. A soft purr escaped him when she rubbed her thumb along his cheek. Without thinking, his rough, sandpaper tongue swept out and ran along her wrist.

His eyes snapped open at her smothered giggle. In the darkness, he could see her eyes shining with delight. He reached out and pulled her into his arms, pressing his face against the curve of her neck and shoulder. He loved her so much.

"Today…, " he began before pausing and raising his head. "I love you. I didn't want you to see me like this."

"I know," she whispered. "Everything will work out."

Sharden reluctantly released her. Turning his back to her, he stared at the flames. No, everything would not be alright. This was the last time he would change. This… This was who he was now. Tomorrow he would be twenty-five and the curse would be permanent.

"There's something I should have told you," he said in a quiet voice. "Tomorrow…." He turned to look at her with regret. "Tomorrow I will be twenty-five. The curse… This time will be different. I will remain a beast. The witch…."

Lisa reached out and touched his arm. "I know what the witch did," she said, silencing him. "I don't care. I love you, Sharden, whether you are a man or a beast or an irritating prince. I fell in love with you, the person inside." She placed her hand over his heart.

Sharden reached down and tenderly cupped her hand in his paw. Lifting it, he pressed the back of it to his mouth. As much as it hurt, he had to make her understand that their being together was impossible now. He started to release her hand, but her fingers curled around his thick paw and she held on to him.

"There can be no future," he insisted.

"On the contrary," she interrupted. "There is nothing but the future."

"Lisa, you don't understand," he growled softly. "It is not safe to live above! The villagers already fear me and they have never seen me in this form. I must spend the rest of my life locked away."

He watched as Lisa looked around the converted cells of the dungeon with a critical look. Her lips twisted and she pressed them together as she turned in a tight circle. When she turned back to stare at him, he knew she was going to twist his words into something positive. The determined light in her eyes and the way she was trying to hide the grin were his first warning.

"This isn't so bad," she said, putting her hands on her hips. "It's actually quite cozy. A little creative lighting, a few more throw rugs and some pictures would do marvels with the place. If we had a nice kitchen over there, your folks could come for dinner on Saturday nights."

Sharden's lip twitched and he shook his head. "Why I thought you'd have a problem with this situation is beyond me," he muttered in exasperation. "Lisa, you must think about this."

"I have," she said with a suddenly serious expression, dropping her arms and stepping close to him again. "I never would have made love with you this afternoon if I'd had any doubts. I'm in this with you, Sharden. For better or for worse, in sickness and in health, till death rips us apart or I strangle you for being so hard-headed."

Sharden reached out and pulled her into his arms. This time, he didn't bother to hide the sharp-tooth grin. "Until you strangle me?" He repeated with a slightly raised eyebrow.

She snorted at him even as her hands rose to cup his cheeks. "If you ever disappear on me like you did earlier, you bet your ass I will," she growled, rising up on her toes to press a kiss to his nose.

Sharden groaned and leaned down and rubbed his cheek against her neck. "I love you, Lisa," he whispered, closing his eyes as a strange dizziness swept over him. "Lisa...."

"Sharden!" Lisa cried out in alarm when she felt him sway. Her arms moved down to wrap around his waist when his knees suddenly collapsed. She steadied him as he sank down to the floor. "Sharden, what's wrong?"

"I... don't know," he muttered as he fell backwards and stared up at her. "I... feel strange."

"Sharden," she whispered his name again, frantically touching his face. "I'll get help. I'll call your father."

"No," he choked. "Don't... leave me."

"I love you," she whispered, stroking his face tenderly with her hands.

A wave of heat rose up in him. He tried to imagine it was Lisa's love causing the heat, but he feared it was something else. Perhaps there had been a part of the curse he was unaware of. His body arched as the moonlight from the windows washed over him. Turning his head, he stared at the shimmering beams. It felt as if it was sucking the life out of him. He weakly raised his hand to catch the tear on Lisa's cheek. His hand froze midway. It was glowing.

The light swirled and twisted, sparkling as it floated upward. In the transparency of the moonbeam, he could see the magic of the witch's spell as it floated upward, as if held a prisoner in the shaft of light as it moved away from his body. Lisa's hand reached out and wrapped around his, threading her fingers through his.

"Lisa!" He exclaimed in a hoarse voice.

"Hold on to me," she choked out. "Don't you dare let go."

Shimmering waves floated upward from his body, lifting him off the cold stone floor. They watched together as the threadlike filaments rose, swirled and disappeared through the open window above. Sharden gasped as the last thread snapped and his body sank back to the ground. Shaken, he gazed up at Lisa's stunned face.

"What...?" He whispered, pushing past his fear.

"I see you," she said softly, lifting his hand and pressing it against her cheek. "I see you, Sharden."

Sharden's eyes moved to where his hand was pressed against her cheek. His hand... not that of the beast. His fingers trembled as he pulled them free. He turned it staring at it in wonder before looking back at Lisa with a growing smile. Their laughter erupted as his arms swept out to wrap around her. Rolling, he stared down at her for a moment before pressing his lips to her in a kiss that held all his love for her in it.

"Forever," he whispered when he pulled back several breathless minutes later.

Lisa smiled up at him. "You bet your ass forever," she swore, wrapping her fingers around his neck. "I still think you were gorgeous before, too."

Sharden laughed, pushing up off the ground with her still holding onto his neck. He rose, pulling her up into his arms as he did. Holding her tightly, his eyes flickered to the moon high above.

"We have the rest of the night for you to tell me how much," he teased.

Lisa sighed and rested her head against his chest. "We have the rest of our lives," she corrected.

Sharden closed his eyes for a brief moment as he hugged her to him. He didn't know if it was her love for him or his for her or the combination of the two that broke the curse. He didn't care. As long as Lisa was with him, they could face anything together. Opening his eyes, he carried her to his bed. Tomorrow would come soon enough to let his parents know the curse had been broken. Tonight was all theirs.

Lowering Lisa down onto the covers, he pressed another kiss to her lips even as his fingers worked on the ribbons holding her dress on. Her fingers were making short work of his shirt. Soon, they were wrapped around each other, dressed in nothing more than the glow of the moonlight and their love.

Epilogue

"Lisa, hurry! It's time," the queen said with a laugh.

Lisa smooth the white silk down over her stomach one more time before she turned and picked up the bouquet of flowers. Swallowing, she nodded. Today was her wedding day. It had been almost two months since that night in the dungeon. Two months that had sped by at an amazing rate. The palace had been open to any and all who wished to attend the wedding of Prince Sharden and Lady Lisa Tootle. The only ones missing were Lisa's adopted family.

"I'm ready," Lisa said, turning and freezing when she saw the queen frozen like a statue by the door. Next to her was a middle aged woman that looked vaguely familiar. "Who are you? What have you done?"

The woman stared at Lisa with wide brown eyes that shimmered with tears. Stepping closer, she raised a trembling hand and touched Lisa's rosy cheek. It took a minute for Lisa to realize why the woman looked so familiar. She looked just like her, only older.

"My beautiful, beautiful little girl," the woman whispered. "For so long, all I could do was watch you from afar."

"Who are you?" Lisa whispered again, this time in a slightly choked voice.

The woman smiled tenderly at Lisa. "I'm your mother," she said in a voice filled with emotion. "Gestasia."

"My mother!" Lisa choked, stepping backwards several feet. "How? Why?"

A sad smile curved Gestasia's lips. "I was a foolish young witch who allowed her anger and bitterness to control her. You were ripped from my arms and cast to the other side of the doorway. I could see you, but never touch."

Lisa frowned as she studied Gestasia's face. The frown cleared as more pieces to the puzzle came together. She had seen this woman once before – at the small hut in the meadow. Only that time, she had been old and wrinkled.

"It was you," she began with a shake of her head.

"Yes," Gestasia said, twisting her hands together and looking away. "I met your young prince shortly after his first change. He wasn't like his parents. He helped me and asked nothing in return. I sent him to the valley where I had planned to raise you. A few months ago, I found hope that there might be a way to break the curse I had cast and bring you home. The young prince came to me again."

"You were old... and you took his gold," Lisa accused, raising her eyebrow at Gestasia.

Gestasia chuckled and nodded. "Even a witch needs money to survive. The first spell ripped you away from me. In anger, I placed another curse on young Sharden. The cost of that spell was my youth," she explained with a sigh.

"Why are you young again?" Lisa asked, puzzled.

"You broke the spell," Gestasia said. "You are from this world, so you could return through the doorway. But, it would take your love for Sharden, no matter what he looked like, to break the spell. With the curse broken, I was also freed."

Lisa looked skeptically at Gestasia. "So, are you expecting some 'Thank you, all's well in the world' hug or acceptance from me or something? I have to tell you, I'm a little upset about the things you've done," Lisa retorted dryly. "Not to mention why didn't you mention any of this before, instead of waiting until my wedding day; which, by the way, I'm late for!"

Gestasia shook her head. "No, I don't expect you to forgive me," she replied with a sad smile. "I just wanted you to know that I'm sorry and that – I love you. I always have."

Lisa shifted uneasily from one foot to the other. Her lips twisted in sardonic amusement. She had to admit, if she looked at the positive side of things, she might not have met Sharden if not for all the misadventures. Glancing at Gestasia under her eyelashes, she finally released an exasperated sigh. She had never been good at holding a grudge.

"How would you like to go to a wedding today? I know this witch's daughter who met this really cool prince," Lisa finally said with a crooked grin. "He might like to meet his mother-in-law. After all, she is the one that turned him into this really gorgeous beast."

"He *was* rather cute, wasn't he?" Gestasia responded with a hopeful smile.

"Yeah, he was," Lisa said. "I think it might be best if you unfroze the queen if we are going to make it in time."

Gestasia nodded. "I have one more gift for you," she said.

"What?" Lisa asked, looking suspiciously at her newly discovered mother.

Gestasia snapped her fingers and a large mirror appeared on the other side with Lisa's adopted family. They were staring at the mirror in awe. All of them erupted into one loud, boisterous group when they saw her.

"Lisa!" Her adopted mom shouted above all the others.

"Mom!" Lisa cried in delight, stepping closer to the mirror. "Mom, I'm getting married!" She twirled around, holding out her arms. "To a prince!"

"We know," her mom laughed, wiping at her tears.

"I couldn't bring them here in the flesh, but I knew you would want them to know that you are happy and safe," Gestasia said, quietly reaching out and touching Lisa's arm in compassion.

Lisa nodded, wiping at the tears threatening to escape. "Do they know? About Sharden? About this world?" She asked, turning to look at her mom and dad. "I love you, guys."

"We know. We love you, too, honey," her dad said. "I'm proud to be called your dad."

"We'll be there watching, luv," her mom promised. "Go knock them out."

"You rock, sis!" Her youngest brother called out from the back. "Send me a sword or something."

"I will if I can," Lisa laughed.

"Time to go," Gestasia replied. "I'll send the mirror to the wedding hall."

Lisa nodded, waving at her adopted family before they disappeared. "By the way, who is my real father?" She asked with a sniff.

Gestasia grinned. "The Breadmaker," she chuckled. "I absolutely love his bread with sweet cream butter."

"Oh!" Lisa whispered in shock.

With a snap of her fingers, the queen resumed moving toward the door as if nothing had happened. The rest of the afternoon passed in a blur for Lisa. She knew her adoptive family was there from the hoots and hollers coming from both sides of the mirror. The Breadmaker walked her down the aisle and gave her hand to Sharden. A huge smile of pride lit his face when he wasn't searching for Gestasia.

She barely remembered exchanging vows with Sharden, but she did remember his kiss and those that followed. It was late evening by the time they were able to sneak away. The sounds of laughter echoed behind them as Sharden lifted her up onto his mount.

"Where are we going?" She asked breathlessly as he settled behind her.

"I know this amazing little valley with a secluded hut that I wanted to take you to," Sharden whispered in her ear before brushing a kiss to her neck.

"What about your parents?" She asked as he tapped his heels to his mount.

"I believe they were going to have a long talk with your mother and father," he said as they rode out the gate.

"What about clothes?" She added when she realized that she was still wearing her wedding dress.

Sharden's husky chuckle echoed through the cool night air. "You won't be needing any if I have anything to do with it," he promised.

Lisa tilted her head back against his shoulder and laughed. The light of the full moon lit their way as they passed through the village and down along the narrow path. It even streamed into the dark recesses of the cave, lighting their way all the way down to the hut. Inside, a nice fire burned in the fireplace and a large selection of fruits, breads, cheeses, and sweet cream butter sat on the table with a large note that said 'In case of emergency'.

"I think I might like having two additional parents," she whispered as Sharden carried her into their bedroom.

"I know I will love their daughter," Sharden replied, laying her down on the bed before covering her lips with his in a long, passion-filled kiss. "Forever."

The End

If you loved this story by me (S. E. Smith) please leave a review. You can also take a look at additional books and

sign up for my newsletter at
http://sesmithfl.com **and**
http://sesmithya.com to hear about my
latest releases or keep in touch using the
following links:

Website: http://sesmithfl.com

Newsletter:
http://sesmithfl.com/?s=newsletter

Facebook:
https://www.facebook.com/se.smith.5

Twitter:
https://twitter.com/sesmithfl

Pinterest:
http://www.pinterest.com/sesmithfl/

Blog:
http://sesmithfl.com/blog/

Forum:
http://www.sesmithromance.com/forum/

Additional Books by S.E. Smith

<u>YA Books</u>

Voyage of the Defiance: Breaking Free series
Dust: Before and After

Paranormal and Science Fiction short stories and novellas

    For the Love of Tia (Dragon Lords of Valdier Book 4.1)

    A Dragonlings' Easter (Dragonlings of Valdier Book 1.1)

    A Dragonlings' Haunted Halloween (Dragonlings of Valdier Book 1.2)

    A Dragonlings' Magical Christmas (Dragonlings of Valdier Book 1.3)

Abducting Abby (Dragon Lords of Valdier: Book 1)

Capturing Cara (Dragon Lords of Valdier: Book 2)

Tracking Trisha (Dragon Lords of Valdier: Book 3)

Ambushing Ariel (Dragon Lords of Valdier: Book 4)

Cornering Carmen (Dragon Lords of Valdier: Book 5)

Paul's Pursuit (Dragon Lords of Valdier: Book 6)

Twin Dragons (Dragon Lords of Valdier: Book 7)

Lords of Kassis Series

River's Run (Lords of Kassis: Book 1)

Star's Storm (Lords of Kassis: Book 2)

Jo's Journey (Lords of Kassis: Book 3)

Ristéard's Unwilling Empress (Lords of Kassis: Book 4)

Magic, New Mexico Series

Touch of Frost (Magic, New Mexico Book 1)

Taking on Tory (Magic, New Mexico Book 2)

Sarafin Warriors

Choosing Riley (Sarafin Warriors: Book 1)

Viper's Defiant Mate (Sarafin Warriors Book 2)

The Alliance Series

Hunter's Claim (The Alliance: Book 1)

Razor's Traitorous Heart (The Alliance: Book 2)

Dagger's Hope (The Alliance: Book 3)

Zion Warriors Series

Gracie's Touch (Zion Warriors: Book 1)

Krac's Firebrand (Zion Warriors: Book 2)

Paranormal and Time Travel Novels

<u>Spirit Pass Series</u>

Indiana Wild (Spirit Pass: Book 1)

Spirit Warrior (Spirit Pass Book 2)

<u>Second Chance Series</u>

Lily's Cowboys (Second Chance: Book 1)

Touching Rune (Second Chance: Book 2)

Excerpts of S. E. Smith Books

If you would like to read more S. E. Smith stories, she recommends <u>Abducting Abby</u>, the first in her Dragon Lords of Valdier Series. Or if you prefer a Paranormal or Time

Travel with a twist, you can check out <u>Lily's Cowboys</u> or <u>Indiana Wild</u>...

About the Author

S.E. Smith is a *New York Times*, *USA TODAY*, *International, and Award-Winning* Bestselling author of science fiction, romance, fantasy, paranormal, and contemporary works for adults, young adults, and children. She enjoys writing a wide variety of genres that pull her readers into worlds that take them away.

59124976R00075

Made in the USA
Charleston, SC
30 July 2016